WINTER WOLF

WINTER WOLF

By

DR BO WAGNER

Word of His Mouth Publishers
Mooresboro, NC

All Scripture quotations are taken from the **King James Version** of the Bible.

ISBN: 978-1-941039-18-2

Printed in the United States of America
©2021 Dr. Bo Wagner

Word of His Mouth Publishers
Mooresboro, NC

www.wordofhismouth.com

Cover art by Chip Nuhrah

CHAPTER ONE

Vacation was behind us, leaving us all in desperate need of a vacation as we made our way up the highway. I know that probably sounds odd, but seeing as how we almost all got blown to smithereens and drowned in the deepest part of the ocean on our vacation, it really isn't.

And while that particular kind of weird is weird to us, weird in general isn't.

Par for the course for my two sisters and me, really. We are the Night Heroes.

I am Kyle Warner, by the way, and I am sixteen years old. My sister Carrie, age fourteen, had her head buried in a book as the lovely scenery of Virginia whipped by, which, if you have read any of our other adventures, does not surprise you. Aly, age thirteen, was engaged in a life-or-death thumb war... against herself. Again, if you have read our other adventures, that kind of thing probably does not surprise you either; she is pure lightning in a bottle and utterly unpredictable. I am pretty sure you could power a decent size city with her if you could harness her energy.

Anyway, weird is not new to us, even though our last adventure was very different. Normally we hear the voice of The Conductor and wake up in the distant past somewhere and are given some dangerous mission to go on for God. This has landed us in places like Nazi Germany, the Battle of Chickamauga, West Virginia more than once, and has had us facing off against bad men in a mine, pirates, knife-wielding Indians, and even The Moth Man. And all of that just barely scratches the surface. But during our last vacation, the danger was in our own time, in waking hours and broad daylight, as terrorists decided to blow up the cruise ship that our family was vacationing on.

After all the time we have been the heroes, mom and Dad were the major heroes in all of that, though we sure helped.

Mom and dad. We always assumed that they had no idea that we were putting our lives in danger time and time again, but now we aren't so sure.

When we wake up in the past, if we get injured in any way, we bring that back with us into our own time. If we ever die... yeah.

We can carry things back into the past with us to help; we just go to sleep with it. When the day in the past is done, we go to sleep back there in time and then wake up in our own time fully rested like we just got a full night's sleep. We never know when the call in the night is going to come; some weeks it does, some weeks it doesn't. But we are always ready.

"Burrrrp!"

Oh, wow. That one from Aly was at least a six and brought a "corrective look" from my mom from the front passenger seat of the trusty old Yukon. Aly just giggled and said, "Don't be jealous!"

Dad ignored it all and kept on driving. He was scheduled to start a revival at the Emmanuel Baptist Church in Abingdon, Virginia, in just a few hours and wanted to get to the hotel in plenty of time for us all to get checked in and freshened up.

My dad is an evangelist. He travels all over the place preaching the Bible, and we all get to come along with him. That means we are homeschooled and take all of our work with us wherever we go. And I would say that that explains Carrie, the genius and historian of our team, having her head in a book, but she reads even when she isn't in school.

Dad has preached at the Emmanuel Baptist Church of Abingdon ever since we Warner Brats (Mom and dad's pet name for us) were little. Up until last year, it was pastored by Bryan Treadway, and we kids were good friends with all of his kids, and he has like a bajillion of them. But the Lord moved him into another work a few months ago, and now Brother Kevin Rogerson is the pastor. We kids have never met him and his family, but dad says they have a bunch of kids too, so were are pretty excited to get there and meet them.

The miles pass pretty quickly when you are whizzing along at seventy miles an hour. And pretty soon, we were turning off of I-26 North onto I-81 North. As we got onto that road, we started passing familiar sights on the left: Bass Pro Shop, hotels, restaurants; it is a booming area, being just outside of Bristol.

A few miles later, we were getting off at exit fourteen, looping back around under the highway, and wheeling into the parking lot of the Comfort Inn and Suites. Then came the standard "people ants" routine that we have perfected for years; checking in, parking, carrying luggage; Dad had everything down to a science.

When we got into the two adjoining rooms, mom took over. She made sure everyone got cleaned up while she ironed clothes. Dad and I took fifteen minutes or so to get fully dressed and ready, then we sat and waited for the next hour while the girls got ready. I have learned not to say a word about that, and dad has possessed that wisdom for years.

Finally, everyone was ready, and we headed out. Back down the hall, take the stairs to the lobby (dad is usually too impatient for elevators) through the lobby, and back into the Yukon. We turned right out of the parking lot, then left at the light just a tenth of a mile or so later, and headed down Lee Highway. A mile or so down the road, way up on the hill, sits the Emmanuel Baptist Church. It is beautiful. It is also located right between an airport and a cemetery. I'm not sure why, but that always strikes me as kind of funny. It's like "going up" on one side and "going down" on the other.

The Yukon wound its way up the curvy drive, past the church on the right, and then up the straight driveway behind the church to the parsonage.

We would be having supper with Pastor Rogerson and his family before service. We pulled up to his garage, piled out, and made our way down the front sidewalk to the door.

A ring of the bell brought Mrs. Rogerson to the door, which she opened wide. With a big smile, she told us to come on in. We could smell the food already, so we didn't have to be asked twice.

CHAPTER TWO

Hannah, Hope, Faith, Caleb, Lydia, Joy, and Olivia. We found out pretty quickly that those were the names of Pastor Rogerson's and Mrs. April's kids. And all of them are just as friendly as can be and made us feel right at home.

Pastors and their families are some of the coolest people on earth. They seem to know instinctively how to make everyone's day. All of us kids got to sit together around a big table in the living room to eat so that we could talk and get to know each other. And the food was "kid-friendly." No offense to things like vegetables and meats and soups, but when a table is also crowded with things like mac and cheese and pizza rolls and corndogs, you know the adults have not forgotten what it is like to be kids.

And so, we happily noshed away, talking about church and school and sports and boys and girls and, of course, our recent "not so vacationy" vacation.

"Dude, seriously? Like, a 'bomb' bomb?" Caleb asked with wide eyes.

"Yep, seriously. Bomb bomb."

Hope chimed in with, "Wow, that's absolutely crazy."

"That's a good way to put it," Carrie said as she took a sip of her Sprite. "I'm just glad things aren't always that crazy."

When she said that (with a straight face, no less) Aly immediately got choked up. Mom looked like she was going to get up and come over to her and give her the Heimlich maneuver, but Aly just held her hand up as if to say, "I'm good, I just need a minute."

I cut my eyes over at Carrie, and she just carried on with her supper with only the slightest grin playing at the corner of her mouth.

We enjoyed a good solid hour of supper and fellowship with Pastor Rogerson and his family, but finally, it was time for the most important thing of all, the church service. Nothing in the world, not even the dangerous, super-secret work my sisters and I do in the past in the middle of the night, is anywhere near as important as telling people about Jesus and of their need for Him. People need to be saved, and He is the only way. So, all of us Warners know to be prayed up and ready for every service; we want God to be able to work through us rather than having to do His work in spite of us.

We all made our way down to the church and came in the back way. We pretty quickly ran into a good number of our friends that we had gotten to know in previous meetings, people like Noah and Joanna and Dallas and a bunch of others. There was a lot of backslapping and handshaking and high-fiving, and catching up on who was now liking who, what church activities everyone had been on, and how everyone's team was doing.

But pretty soon, we heard the piano start to play, and we knew it was time to begin the service. So we all made our way into the lovely auditorium and found seats near the back.

The song leader called out the number of a hymn for us, and everyone in the place stood and began to sing. At the risk of sounding like some kind of an oldster, I absolutely love the old, traditional church hymns. There is just something about the words and the truth and even the sound of things like "Amazing Grace" and "The Old Rugged Cross" and "How Firm A Foundation" and "Victory In Jesus" that makes me happy to be a Christian.

Everyone in the place sang from the bottom of their hearts, and as the sound filled the room, it was in lovely four-part harmony.

After a couple of songs and a couple of prayers, the pastor stood and welcomed everyone to the service, gave some announcements, and then invited the choir up to sing. Emmanuel has a huge choir, and it is really good. They sang three songs and did a great job on all of them. Then they came down, an offering was taken for my dad, and a group of three sweet ladies came up to sing a couple of special songs.

And then it was time for the preaching.

My dad almost always tries to be very encouraging in his preaching, even though he will absolutely scald sin and warn of the judgment to come as necessary. But especially early in a week of revival, he usually tries to preach something to encourage those who are hurting or discouraged. And tonight was no exception. He preached one of his newer messages called "God's Way Always Makes Sense... Eventually."

In that message, he always picks some kid to be Joshua and go around and around the city of Jericho. This time it was a guy named Daniel who did a fantastic job running around one of the sections of pews thirteen times by the time the message was over. The point of the message is that had they stopped anywhere along the way, this odd plan of God never would have made sense because they never would have seen the walls fall.

There was a lot more to it than that, and as usual, during the invitation, the altars were packed with people praying, and some of them softly crying. I know I'm still pretty young, but it seems to me that a lot of people are carrying a lot of very big burdens.

The service came to a close, and Pastor Rogerson and his family took all of us Warners over to McDonald's by the hotel for some ice cream and fellowship. We had a great time for about an hour, then finally said our goodbyes, and made our way back to the Comfort Suites.

Our family prayer and conversation time was now over. Mom and dad were in their room bedding down for the night; we three kids were in our adjoining room also getting ready for sleep – or for whatever else the night may hold.

"So, this is our first stop since our vacation/not vacation. Do you think all of that changed anything for us?"

"What you mean, Aly?" I asked, though I was pretty sure I knew where she was headed with that.

"Well, I mean, come on, none of that was exactly normal. And there is still the question as to how much, if anything, mom and dad know."

"No, it definitely wasn't normal," Carrie chimed in, "and no, we still don't know what we would all really like to know about mom and dad. But the way we should probably look at it is that God came through for us. He sent help when we needed it. And even though that was just 'normal' trouble in the present, if there even is such a thing, we stepped up to the plate like we were supposed to."

14

That last reference made me raise my eyebrows and grin a bit.

"Stepped up to the plate? Since when do you use sports references?" I asked with good humor.

"Hey, we all learn and grow, okay, bro? Who knows, one day you might even start using science references!"

"Ow, that hurts!" I said, but I was laughing as I did so.

As my laughter subsided, though, everything just sort of naturally got quiet. No, none of us knew if we would get a call in the night. None of us knew, if we did get that call, if things would go back to being "normal" or at least our weird version of normal.

But I knew that all of us were on the same page on the one thing that mattered; whatever call came, if any, we Night Heroes would answer it.

CHAPTER THREE

"Hey, if you kids are going to be part of this wagon train, I would recommend you wake up and get in line like everybody else."

I knew the voice before my eyes even popped open. I also knew from the sound of all the other voices around us that we were starting this adventure in the midst of a bunch of other people and that our Conductor was pretending like he did not know us because of that.

I quickly opened my eyes and looked off to my right and saw Carrie sitting up on the old wooden bench. Then to my left, ditto for Aly. We knew that we could not talk much at that moment; people were indeed milling all around us, and the Conductor was standing in front of us looking stern.

I knew that Carrie was taking in every detail with her eyes, trying to figure out the when and the where.

I also knew already, though, that the when was a very long time ago, maybe further back than we had ever been.

We stood up to face our Conductor, and though the look on his face was still stern, the characteristic friendliness was still shining in his eyes. He motioned to the left with a nod of his head, and we began to follow him through a crowd of people. But this was not a crowd of people coming out of the buildings of the town because there was no town, unless you count exactly one building, a tavern, as a town. Off in the distance, I could see a log fort and the beginnings of a few log houses inside of that fort.

Other than that, there was nothing, though I did see smoke rising from various places in the hills where there were probably cabins with chimneys.

So, where in the world was this crowd of people from? This was just a dirt road with a couple of benches beside it and wagons gathering in from who knows where.

I could see that we were now in line and that the line of people led to some guy sitting on a stump outside the tavern speaking to people, taking money from them, and writing something down in a little book. It was clearly going to take us a few minutes to get to him, so I stepped up beside the Conductor and whispered, "How have you been, sir?"

He grinned ever so slightly and whispered back, "Oh, you know, pretty good. I mean, not 'luxurious cruise with explosive ending' kind of good, but, good."

"Har, har, very funny," Carrie quipped from the other side of him. "Maybe next time you could come along on vacation with us, you know, just in case!"

He actually laughed out loud at that, but then as other people turned to look at him, he quickly choked all of that back. Whatever was going on, this did not seem like a jolly, share-a-good-laugh kind of moment.

Everyone went back to what they were doing, and he spoke again, this time in a lower whisper than before.

"As you can see, we aren't exactly getting to start this mission in some quiet place that will allow you to take the time and preplan what you will do. But as quietly as we can, why don't we start the way we normally do? What do you think, Carrie; time and place?"

True to form, my brainiac sister did not even hesitate.

"Late fall or early winter, a bit after 1780, Black's Fort. Or as we will know it in our day, Abingdon, Virginia."

The Conductor smiled. "Well done, as usual, young lady. Why don't you fill your siblings in on how you arrived at that conclusion?"

"Okay. Well, Abingdon is the easy part, since the lay of the land is identical with everything that we saw yesterday in our own day, and the handful of red and orange and yellow leaves on all of the mostly barren trees are the dead giveaway as to the time of year.

"The fact that no real town is here immediately puts it back at least in the late-1700s. But the smoke rising at four or five places from chimneys off in the distance puts it after 1765 when the first six settlers bought land from Dr. Thomas Walker to settle the place. And the fort was built by Thomas Black in 1774 to protect the area from attack by the Cherokee. That tavern was built in 1779. Lastly, the road we are on, since it is starting right here near Bristol, must be the foot trail blazed by Daniel Boone himself in 1774 going through the Cumberland Gap and into Kentucky, and it is called the Wilderness Road. But it is now obviously wide enough for pack animals, and that widening was done in 1780 by a man named John Kincaid.

"That fort down there, by the way, is obviously why they called this place, or, 'call this place' Black's Fort."

"Or Wolf's Hill, depending on who you ask," came a deep male voice, followed by the sound of tobacco spit splattering on the ground.

We jerked just a little bit and turned ever so slightly to see a leathery-looking bearded man who had just walked up beside us in time to overhear Carrie's last words.

"Back about 15 year' ago, fella named Daniel Boone was out this way doin' some huntin'. Pack o' wolves come outta that cave over there and attacked his dogs, killed a couple of 'em. Most folks have called this place Wolf's Hill ever since, though quite a few have done took to callin' it Black's Fort, like you said."

I extended my hand to the man and said, "Kyle, Kyle Warner. And this is my sister Carrie, and this is my sister Aly."

The man clasped my hand, shook it firmly, and as he did, I saw his eyes widen a good bit. At sixteen years old, I am already a bit over six feet tall, as strong as a bull, and I shake hands accordingly.

He nodded and said, "Look forward to havin' you with us on the trail. A good strong young man like yerself can be of use huntin' and standin' watch against injuns, and the girls can help cook and clean."

Oh boy.

I did not even have to look over at either of my sisters to know that both of them had steam coming out of their ears and faces that looked as angry as a librarian with a library full of screaming cheerleaders.

The man turned around and walked off, and Aly said, "I don't know his name yet, but I think I'll just call him 'Lucky.'"

"Lucky?" I said, just a touch surprised. "I was expecting something much harsher."

"What she doubtless means by that, my imperceptive brother, is that whatever our mission is, that man will be lucky to live through it to the end of the week."

I just nodded a couple of times as if to say, "Ah. Gotcha."

"I do hate to interrupt your musings on how to kill your new friend and bury the body," the Conductor said, "but we only have a couple of more minutes in this line, so we need to talk about the situation and whether or not you intend it to be a part of it."

"As if we ever wouldn't?" Carrie said flatly.

"I understand, and I appreciate that," he said, "but it behooves you to know that each and every time, you do have a choice. Again, God never makes anyone's choices for them, be it the choice for salvation, or the choice to serve Him or not, or any other choice."

"Got it, sir," I said. "So, what exactly is the mission?"

He grinned and replied, "As has sometimes been the case before, I am not entirely sure. All I know is that this wagon train will be leaving from here in just a bit, and the eventual destination is, in fact, Kentucky. The far side of Kentucky, actually, Louisville, right on the banks of the Ohio River. These folks are heading west looking for a better life, which to them means good crop land, good hunting grounds, easily available salt, and plentiful, cheap property. Unlike your time in Rogersville, Tennessee, where there was a little boy to rescue from an Indian warrior or your time off of the coast of North Carolina where a town was being terrorized by pirates, I do not know of a single problem or issue in this time or place that presently needs to be dealt with.

"But God always knows what He is doing, and for whatever reason, He wants you to be a part of this particular procession.

"So, if you choose to join this mission having no more information to go on than that, but knowing that, as always, it could be dangerous or even deadly, just keep standing in this line.

"But if you choose to say no, just slip out of the line and hike off into the trees aways. Rest the day away, go to sleep tonight, and, as always, you will wake back up safely in your own time."

"Is there even really a question here?" Aly asked with mock annoyance.

"Not from me," I said.

"Or from me," Carrie finished.

"Good. You three never disappoint," the Conductor said with a smile. "Now then, since you are all in, listen very carefully and quickly to what I have to say. When we get to the man with the ledger book, I am going to pay the fare for all three of you since I think it reasonable to assume that none of you have any money that will work in the year 1785."

"You're not wrong," Carrie said with mild sarcasm.

The Conductor continued. "Once I have paid your fare, you three need to come with me a little way into the trees where I have some supplies waiting for you. As Carrie observed, it is late in the year, and therefore will be getting extremely cold at night. So, I have era-appropriate coats and other boxes of needed supplies for you to load into whatever wagon you ride in."

The three of us just nodded. We did not know *what* we were here for, but we knew *Who* we were here for. And just a few moments later, once our Conductor had left us, we Night Heroes knelt to speak to that *Who*.

CHAPTER FOUR

I guess that probably no kids from our modern day could really wrap their minds around what it would be like for there to not be any roads. I mean like actual roads, asphalt and concrete. But we were presently bouncing along in the back of an old-fashioned-wagon was, in the technical sense of the word, a road. But in our day, the kindest word that anybody would apply to it would be "path."

"Ouch!" Aly said as the back of her head slammed, yet again, onto one of the wooden hoops holding the wagon's cover in place.

Carrie just looked at her, closed her eyes and shook her head softly back and forth, and said, "You know, after about the fifth time of that happening, it seems like you might figure out that it would be a good idea to move down a foot or so."

"Oh yeah, I guess that would work," Aly shrugged, and then slid a bit to her right. We had been on the trail for about an hour, and thus far we had the entire back of this particular wagon to ourselves. A man who was probably about thirty but looked more like fifty was driving the wagon. Conditions in the wilderness of old were not exactly conducive to a person staying youthful looking into their adulthood.

Beside the man, though, was his wife. And I sort of felt like she may have been pretty in an old-fashioned, plain sort of way if she had not also been sick. I did not know what was wrong with her, but her face was drawn and pale, and she coughed way too often for it to be anything good. To make matters worse, she was also clearly a young mother, and the baby that she was clutching didn't sound any too healthy either.

"That poor baby cries so weakly," Aly said, "I wish mom were here; she would know what to do to make him better."

"There aren't exactly any drugstores or even Walmarts to get any medicine from out here," Carrie said sadly, "I don't know that even mom could do anything under these circumstances."

We sort of fell silent at that, and the rocking of the wagon soon put Aly to sleep.

Just a few minutes later, though, the lady and her baby joined us in the back of the wagon, and Aly woke right back up when I greeted her.

"Good afternoon, Mrs. Susan, and thank you again for allowing my sisters and me to join you and your family in your wagon."

She smiled weakly but pleasantly and said, "It is our distinct pleasure, young man. Please, though, tell me your names again?"

"Gladly. I am Kyle, this is Carrie, and the sleepyhead waking up beside you is Aly."

Aly grinned up at her, wiggled her fingers, and said, "Hey! And what a pretty baby you have!"

The woman beamed from ear to ear at that.

"Thank you, sweetheart; I appreciate that. This is Thomas, and he is three months old today."

"If you don't mind me asking," I said, "what made you and your husband decide to risk such a long and dangerous trip? I hope I'm not being inappropriate by saying this, but you and Thomas both seem a little bit, well, under the weather."

"We'll be fine," she said firmly, "especially once we make it to Louisville. We want Thomas to have a chance to grow up in an area where he can really make something of himself. There is a world of opportunity for anyone willing to brave the road west, and we are willing."

Somehow her answer did not surprise me. People in my day, I guess, would probably never understand the fierceness and independence of the pioneer spirit. But it is that very spirit that helped to tame a land and make America great.

We rode along in silence for a while longer, and then suddenly, the silence was broken when Mrs. Susan took a bad coughing spell. Immediately Carrie and Aly were hovering over her and little Thomas, trying anything they could to make things better. As if instinctively, that young mother handed the baby to Aly and curled up into a ball in Carrie's lap as Carrie held her tightly.

How in the world were they going to survive a trip like this?

I could feel the wagon leaning forward by that point, and I knew we were starting down into a valley and that there would likely be a stream or river to cross at the bottom of it. There would doubtless be dozens of those along the way.

The high-growing sagebrush and the low-hanging branches of the trees on either side of the path were dragging along the sides of the wagon and slapping the wagon's cover as we went. It seemed like nature itself was trying to rip the wagon apart, and I knew that the other fifteen wagons in our sixteen-wagon train were experiencing the exact same thing. It was also getting colder by the minute – way colder, actually. I reached into the wooden chest that the Conductor had provided for us and pulled out some heavier coats for us to wear.

"Are these, like, real fur?" Aly asked as her eyes grew wide.

"Of course, they are, Sis," I said, "I mean, think of where and when we are," I said as I stared hard into her eyes.

Her eyes got wider as well, and I knew that she got the message. We didn't exactly need to be acting surprised at something that was absolutely common to literally everybody in that day.

"Thank you for holding the baby," Mrs. Susan said as she finally sat up out of Carrie's lap, "I can take him from you now."

"Why don't you just let me hold him for a while, and you get some rest," Aly said sweetly, "I don't mind holding him, and I think his mommy could use a break."

"You are too sweet, child, and I thank you. I believe I will indeed take you up on your offer," she said, and then she moved up against the front of the wagon, wrapped herself in a blanket, and was almost instantly fast asleep, albeit a very fitful sleep.

"Um, Kyle, we sort of need to talk, don't you think?" Carrie whispered.

I nodded my head. "I know what you're thinking," I whispered back. "Don't worry. When night falls, they will doubtless stop all of the wagons to make camp. We will offer to go outside the camp and be on watch. That will give us the excuse we need to disappear for the night and show back up again the next morning. They will doubtless have others on watch as well, so everyone should be safe even if we aren't actually there to be on watch.

Carrie nodded, and Aly just ignored us as she continued to rock the baby. He was settling down some and yet still crying weakly.

We finally came to the bottom of the valley, and, sure enough, I could hear the sloshing of the water as the horses' feet followed by the wagon wheels cut through what was obviously a wide yet shallow creek. We came out on the other side and started upward, and as we did, I stepped over Mrs. Susan and out onto the front bench with her husband, Arthur.

He did not look over at me, but simply nodded his head as if in acknowledgment of my presence. He seemed to have both hopefulness and anxiousness etched into every weatherworn line on his face.

"Will be camping just at the top of that plateau," he said simply as he pointed up ahead.

At the rate we were traveling, I guessed that it would take about an hour to get all of the wagons up there. The temperature was continuing to drop, and I pulled my coat closer around my neck and face.

"Are you good, boy?" He asked.

"Yes sir, thank you, I'm fine. How about you? Do you need me to give you a spell on the reins?"

"Naw, just sit back and enjoy the ride; I've got this," he said.

As we climbed ever gradually upward, the trees fell away behind us, and the hill became a meadow of wild grass. The sun was lowering in the sky, and I guessed that it was probably around 4 o'clock in the afternoon. But the clouds were also racing in, and it seemed to me that we would not see a sunset on this day.

"Snow clouds," he said simply.

"That's not so good, I would think."

He just laughed a bit. "It is still early in the winter; it'll probably not be too bad."

Oh, how very wrong that was going to turn out to be.

CHAPTER FIVE

The knock on the solid wooden door between our two rooms jolted we sleepy-headed Night Heroes out of our slumber.

"Breakfast in thirty minutes, Warner brats," dad shouted through the door. "We'll see you in the lobby, don't be late."

"Dibs on the bathroom," Carrie said as her feet hit the floor, and she started heading that way. Presently I could hear the buzz of the electric toothbrush as she began her morning routine.

"Do you think they're okay?" Aly asked as she looked up at me from their bed.

"I think so, Squirt," I said without much concern. "The snow was falling pretty good by the time we bugged out, so I doubt seriously if any raiding Indian parties are going to be a problem. My only concern is how sick Mrs. Susan and the baby seem to be. I can't imagine having a three-month-old on a wagon train in weather like that. I hope they were able to stay plenty warm last night."

A few minutes later, Carrie was dressed and out of the restroom, and Aly took her place. Carrie and I took that time to read a little bit in our Bibles as we do each morning and to pray for a few minutes. And then Aly was out, and I got ready.

And then it was down the stairs and into the hotel dining room for sausage and eggs and biscuits and oatmeal. Ya gotta hand it to most hotel kitchens; they are really, really good!

All five of us got our breakfast to the table, and then we bowed our heads together to pray over the meal as a family. I know that not everyone does that anymore – but everyone should. God gives us every good thing, including our meals, so why shouldn't we be grateful and say thank you?

"I appreciate seeing you folks pray together," a sweet lady who worked at the hotel said as she passed by.

"Thank you kindly, ma'am," dad said pleasantly.

Breakfast passed pleasantly with seconds, and in my case, thirds.

"Sweetie, you might want to slow down," mom said with some concern, "we want you to be able to walk, not to have to be rolled."

The girls laughed, and I was about to answer, but dad beat me to it since I had food in my mouth.

"Don't worry about that, Babe; our first stop for the day is Sugar Hollow Park."

None of us needed to ask what that meant; all of us have been there many times. Sugar Hollow State Park was about ten miles back down the road toward Bristol. It is probably one of my favorite places to run. There are trails leading up into the hills and through beautiful spacious pine forests and around wetlands and over a dam. If you are ever up there, don't miss it, even if you just walk through it.

Within just a few minutes, we were dressed for the occasion and ready to go. We made our way there, parked down by the ballfield, and mom set her watch to track our progress. You may think that we would each have to do that, or that the guys would do it and the girls would do it, but that is absolutely not the case with our family. All of us run and run well. Mom and dad have made sure that we all eat right and stay active. Dad says, "Your body is a gift to you from God. What you do with it is a gift from you to God. Treat it well so that you can serve Him very effectively and for a very long time."

And away we went. Up the winding sidewalk behind the ball field and then onto the dirt path that made its way into the trees.

There are actually several different trails you can take in that park, so the scenery does not ever have to get old. Dad seemed to know them all by heart, and he led the way. I brought up the rear, not because I am slower than anyone, but because dad has taught me to always put the ladies between us so that if there is any danger coming from the front or rear, it has to get through us first to get to them.

That's my dad, always the gentleman.

We ran at a steady, measured pace and went for two hours and twenty minutes. Mom's watch said that we went six and a half miles in that time.

Needless to say, we were all tired and hungry by then.

Rather than going back to the hotel and showering off, then going out again for lunch, we just ran through the nearby Bojangles and ate lunch in the vehicle. Then it was back to the hotel and much-needed showers all around.

And then all of us settled in to do some desk work, with the girls and I working on our schoolwork, mom working on some things for the home, and dad studying for messages. Dad never gets lazy at that. He gets pretty ill at evangelists who have just a small handful of messages that they memorize and recycle year after year after year. "If pastors have the character to study for new messages all the time, evangelists should too," he always says.

We all studied the afternoon away, and then about four o'clock, we started getting ready. By five o'clock, we were sitting in Pastor and Sister Rogerson's home again, this time eating a lovely beef stew and a bunch of different vegetables and homemade biscuits that Faith made. And when we topped those biscuits off with apple butter, man, heaven!

Finally, we wrapped up the meal, sat around and talked for a while, and then headed on down to the church. Folks started drifting in one by one, and then at 6:45, it was time for prayer room again. Everyone poured out their hearts to the Lord, asking Him to do something great during the service. And that is the way it should always be. Mom says we should never feel like we have arrived and no longer need God's help!

As usual, the service was good. Really good. Dad preached a very encouraging message called "After This, Job Lived." And once again, at the invitation, the altar was filled with people crying and pouring out their hearts to God and getting the help they needed to go on.

God is good. I mean, He is really good. And I don't know what everyone else was thinking about, but that is what I went to bed that night thinking about after our family conversation and prayer time.

CHAPTER SIX

There was no call from The Conductor this morning; it was the cold of the snow on my cheek that woke me up. Yikes, what a terrible way to start a morning! I sat up and shook myself off; then I shook Carrie awake on my left and Aly awake on my right.

"Ewwwww," Aly said with undisguised disgust. "Yuck!"

"What gives, Littlest Sister, I thought you love snow?"

"I love playing in the snow, Kyle, not waking up in it."

"It could be worse," Carrie said, "the average mean temperature this time of year in the Arctic Circle is..."

"Shut it, Mega-Mind," Aly said curtly. "Even the polar bears don't care about that."

I heard her, but not exactly. I was straining to hear a distant sound that worried me greatly.

"Shhhh, you two be quiet for a second."

They knew I would never shush them unless it was absolutely necessary, so they instantly fell quiet and began to listen along with me. And in just a few seconds, we all locked eyes and said, "Back to camp, now!"

We were only about a quarter of a mile into the trees, so it did not take us long at all running at top speed through the snow to break out into the open and realize that something had gone horribly wrong in the night.

"There are some of our sentries now!" a chubby and very angry man pointed and said, "just about as worthless as all the rest of them!"

We ignored the insult; we knew that whatever was wrong, we didn't have time for personal battles at that moment.

"Is Mrs. Susan and the baby okay?" I asked frantically.

"Oh, they're fine, just fine," said Lucky, the tobacco spitter from yesterday, "except for the fact that if they live, they'll have to live with the guilt of having caused their man's death."

Mrs. Susan suddenly appeared from around the corner of the wagon and absolutely walloped Lucky with a slap across the face, shrieking, "Shut your mouth! Shut your filthy mouth this instant!" Lucky, apparently not too keen about being embarrassed in front of the rest of the men, immediately raised his hand and swung it towards her face intending to pay her back and slap her to the ground.

I made sure that didn't happen.

I caught his arm by the wrist in midair and held it like it was in a vice.

Stunned, he looked over at me with cold fury and said, "If you want to live to see the end of this day, boy, you need to let go of my arm."

This man was not my enemy, and I knew it. Something horrible had happened in the night, and everyone was on edge. I didn't need to escalate the situation; I needed to defuse it and find out what was going on.

"I'll be glad to do so, sir," I said as humbly as I could, "but if you need someone to strike, I would be much obliged if you would choose me instead of this dear lady. Can we agree to that?"

I saw his face soften, and he quietly said, "I'm not gonna hit you or her. And I apologize for losin' my temper."

I nodded and let his wrist go. Then I said, "Thank you, that means the world to me. Now could you please tell me what happened?"

"It's best that I show you; otherwise, it would be almost impossible to believe."

And then he began to walk toward the back of the wagon that we had just been riding in yesterday. He pulled up short a few feet away from it, pointed at the ground, and simply said, "Look."

I did.

And I had a hard time believing what I was seeing.

The ground was covered with wolf tracks – but that was not the shocking part. The shocking part was that one set of those tracks was absolutely enormous.

I turned to look at Lucky, and he said, "In all of my years, I have never seen any wolf, anywhere, that could fill out those tracks. Most wolves range from four to six feet in length and are around a hundred pounds. On very rare occasions, you might find one that is one hundred twenty pounds. Based on the size of this one's paws and the length of its stride, this monster is probably eight feet long and two hundred fifty pounds or more. And that's not all..."

He nodded to me, and we went around to the back end of the wagon.

"Like every man in this wagon train, he had his family on the inside of the wagon up against the front, and he was laying here at the back end to protect them from anything that would try to get in. And, like every man here, if there had been so much as a sound of any type made, he would have heard it and instantly been awake.

"Wolves are not quiet creatures. Especially not when there is a pack of them this size. But this entire pack snuck past all of our sentries without making a sound, made its way to this wagon specifically, and the monster leading them put his paws right up here" (and he pointed to two marks on the edge of the wagon as he said that) "grabbed a full-grown, 200-pound man by the neck, and dragged him off into the night without making so much as a sound. We followed the drag marks a mile or more off into the trees across the way and finally lost all trail when they dragged his body into the river and came out who knows where upstream or downstream."

I did not have to ask how he knew the wolf had grabbed Susan's husband by the neck. If he had grabbed him in any other spot, the man could have cried out, and people would have known what was happening. I had no doubt in my mind that the wolf crushed his neck instantly. He died without even knowing what was happening.

The man squared up to me and looked me in the eyes. "That devil and all his pack were attracted by the sound of that sick baby crying last night."

He did not have any malice in his voice this time as he said that. And I knew that, whether I liked it or not, it was almost certainly true. And that certainty made me fear what decisions might be made next.

As if he was reading my mind, the man said, "We ought to put them out in the snow right now and leave them behind. But right now, the rest of our womenfolk would make our lives as miserable as Hades if we tried," he said with a very forced smile. "So, my question to you is, can you drive a wagon, and can you drive it hard? We intend to use the daylight hours to put so many miles between us and those wolves that they couldn't catch up with us if they were riding on the wings of devils."

"I can drive the wagon, sir. Just make sure you don't slow down any, or I might just have to pass you," I said with a confident air that was entirely fake.

He just smiled and said, "Good. Load everything up. We leave right away."

In the midst of Carrie and me frantically loading everything up while Aly tended to a basket case of a mother/widow and a sick baby, Carrie asked, "Can you seriously drive this wagon? I mean, I know you did so for a few minutes in Charleston when we were rescuing Mabel from Feeney the Fetid *(A reference from book eight, Runaway), but that was on cobblestone streets, not out in the wilderness."

"We'll find out, I guess," I said. "I paid pretty close attention last night while I was sitting up front with the Mister, just in case."

"Wow, that absolutely does not inspire any confidence, Bro."

"No argument there, Sis. But we honestly don't have much of a choice, do we? There is no way that sick little mama can drive this wagon, so if I don't, they will simply leave her behind and be glad to be rid of her."

Carrie nodded, and we finished loading the campfire utensils and horse feed bags from the previous night. And no sooner had we gotten the last item and Susan and baby Thomas and Aly into the back of the wagon, I heard Lucky shout from somewhere way up front, "Roll out, and roll hard!"

And boy, did we ever.

All that day, every single wagon was pushed double-time; I did not think the horses were going to survive. But it was for their own good as well. If those wolves managed to pick off all the people, the horses would surely be next.

The further we went, the higher my confidence got. I did not know if God had called us here simply for me to drive this wagon to outrun that wolf and those wolves, but it sort of made sense. I really did not see any way that those wolves, creatures of the night, could catch up to us during the night when we were putting so many miles between us and them during the day.

In the midst of it all, I had to admit that the terrain was wild but lovely. Even to this day, the mountains of Virginia and Tennessee are breathtaking. But in the late 1700s, with great stands of virgin forests, they were even more so, especially in the freshly fallen snow.

"Some of those trees must be four and five hundred years old," Carrie said as she slipped up beside me.

"No doubt about that, Sis. How is Mrs. Susan and baby Thomas doing?"

"Not so good, really," Carrie shrugged. "That lady has lost her husband, her best friend, on top of being sick and having a sick baby and racing through the wilderness knowing that they are being chased by wolves. She is a wreck. But at least right now, she is a sleeping wreck; Aly has Thomas and has gotten him quiet enough for her to sleep."

I nodded, and we continued to race on in silence as the horses' hooves tore up chunks of snow and dirt as they powered us forward. And all the while, I was praying, and I knew that

Carrie was, too. When it gets right down to it, all any of us can do is all that we can do; but praying gives us access to what God can do.

The day began to slip away, and the sun touched the horizon as we topped a hill. All of the other wagons pulled up to a stop, and without anyone having to be told, everyone arranged them in a circle.

"Make camp!" came a shout from someone up ahead, "and set sentries!"

Carrie and I made our way into the back of the wagon, and Aly was waking Mrs. Susan.

"Oh, children, you should have awakened me. There was no need for you to do all the work today. Besides, Thomas no doubt has needed feeding for a while."

Aly handed that sweet mother her baby, and Carrie and I looked at each other in the eyes. The fact that that young child had not cried for his mother's milk for so long was not a good thing. Not at all.

We Night Heroes stepped out of the wagon and looked around to decide which part of the trees were going to disappear into to "be sentries" or, as we would put it, take our nightly ride home. About that moment, two older men

50

made their way over there and said, "Go on and set watch. We have already prayed about it and decided to protect this mom and baby during the night. Seems like the least we can do for them after all Jesus done for us."

I tipped my hat and said, "Much obliged, men."

And then we Night Heroes made our way into the trees, praying with all of our hearts that we had gone far enough during the day to avoid any more tragedy during the night.

CHAPTER SEVEN

We went to sleep in the snow and the cold and woke up in the comfort and warmth of our hotel room. I was the first one awake, and I just sort of laid there on my back for a while in my bed, looking up at the ceiling and praying. I really wanted the revival to go well; I also really wanted a mama and baby that no one in our day would ever meet to be safe.

The girls started to stir, and Carrie's feet finally hit the floor as she made her way to the restroom to get ready and prepare for the day. Aly was next, then me, and mom and dad were pleasantly surprised when they knocked on our door and found us all up and dressed and ready for breakfast.

We made our way downstairs, spoke to the nice lady behind the desk and wished her a good day, and made our way out into the trusty old Yukon. We drove back down toward Bristol and stopped in at Perkins and had an amazing breakfast. We downed eggs and bacon and sausage and hash browns and pancakes and waffles. One thing we Warners can do is eat!

As we ate, mom and dad talked a little bit about the news and other grown-up things, and then dad turned his attention to the day at hand.

"So, what would you kids like to do today?" He asked.

"Me, me, me! Ask me!" Carrie said excitedly.

We all busted out laughing at that; normally, she is way more reserved than that.

"Okay, Hunny Bunny, I'll bite; what are you so excited about? What is it that you want to do?"

"I want to go into the actual town part of Abingdon and look around, but I specially want us to go to the Barter Theater," she said excitedly.

"Um, okay," mom said, "what exactly is that? I'm guessing that you already know based on your excitement level."

"Okay, class, sharpen your pencils and pay attention," Carrie said as she assumed a professorial tone. "The linguistic derivation of the word barter..."

"English, please!" Aly interjected with obvious irritation.

Carrie huffed.

"Fine, then. Bartering is when people trade goods or services instead of paying for them with money. The Barter Theatre opened in 1933, during the middle of the Great Depression. It was a crazy idea, really. Since people did not have money to spend on their bills or even their needs, much less on nonessentials like entertainment, theaters around the country went out of business, and actors had no work.

"But a guy named Robert Porterfield decided to start a theater where people could pay for their tickets with crops or livestock, and those crops or livestock is what the actors themselves would work for. It was literally actors bartering entertainment for stuff that they could not buy, and people bartering stuff they could not sell for entertainment that they could not pay for in money.

"Everyone thought the idea was nuts. But it turned out to be wildly successful and is still running to this day nearly a century later.

"And right now, they are actually doing Frankenstein!"

All of us busted out laughing again. Leave it to my brainiac sister to get excited over something like Frankenstein in the theater.

Carrie showed mom and dad what she was talking about on her phone. She and I had just gotten phones for the first time after the cruise ship fiasco. Aly knew that she would still have to wait another year or so to get one.

"Welp, Abingdon and the Barter Theatre it is," dad said matter-of-factly.

Downtown Abingdon, Virginia, is a truly lovely place steeped in history. Many of the sidewalks that line the streets are of very old, hand-laid brick. (Picture of that). Many of the buildings are so old and historical that they have signs in front of them, including two that were noteworthy to we Night Heroes. One because of how well it proved Carrie's brilliance yet again, and the other because of the spiritual legacy it holds. Here, let me show you the one that Carrie was so pleased over.

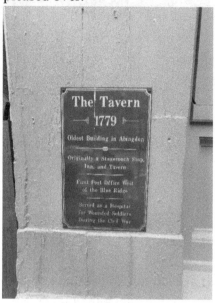

Yep. Built in 1779, just like she said. I never ceased to be amazed at my genius, brainiac sister. But here is the second one that we were so impressed with, the one with the great spiritual legacy.

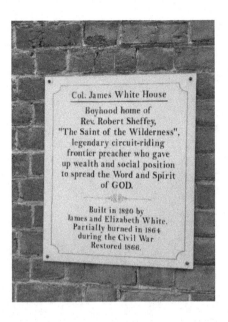

Col. James White House

Boyhood home of
Rev. Robert Sheffey,
"The Saint of the Wilderness",
legendary circuit-riding
frontier preacher who gave
up wealth and social position
to spread the Word and Spirit
of GOD.

Built in 1820 by
James and Elizabeth White.
Partially burned in 1864
during the Civil War
Restored 1866.

If you do not know the story of Sheffey, you really need to watch the movie. He was one of the most powerful preachers who ever lived, and God used him in the most amazing ways. I wondered if the people of Abingdon today really knew what a legacy they had in him having lived there.

There was a lot more to Abingdon as well, much of it dealing with American history.

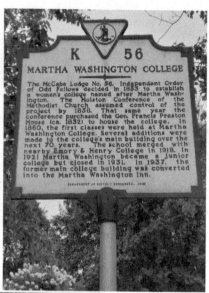

But finally, we came to Carrie's treasure, the Barter Theatre. To her great delight, they had an afternoon showing of Frankenstein. So dad bought tickets for all of us, and then we went exploring more of the town.

And one spot we came to quickly turned our moods a bit dark.

As dad and mom were reading it, Carrie leaned over to me and whispered, "It seems that that devil wolf, or least his buddies, have been doing their thing around here for a long time."

"That makes sense," I whispered back. "Have you paid attention to how prominent wolves still are in this town? There are sculptures and paintings of them everywhere."

"I was noticing that," Aly whispered as well. "But these modern works of art almost make them seem cuddly and likable. I would suspect that a grieving widow we know would dispute that sweet characterization."

Carrie and I just nodded silently at that.

Once mom and dad were done reading the sign, we all went to lunch at a great Mexican restaurant there in Abingdon, the Puerto Nuevo Fresh Mex And Seafood. Pastor Rogerson and his family met us there, and we had a great time of fellowship. Their kids are such a blast, especially the youngest, Olivia. We learned pretty quickly that she loves strawberries and anything pink. Hannah, their oldest, is studying to be a nurse. Aly thought that was really cool since that is what she wants to be when she grows up. Even at her young age, she actually reads books about it.

Oh, in case you go, the Puerto Nuevo has an amazing salsa bar as well. Dad, bless his iron stomach, mixed so many of the different hot salsas together that he probably could have started a motorboat with it.

Once lunch was done, we headed over to the Barter Theatre to watch the show. I have to admit, I was pretty skeptical going into it – but it was absolutely epic. I won't ruin it for you by giving you a bunch of spoiler alerts, but it was really, really good.

Once it was done, though, we headed straight back to the hotel. Dad wanted a little bit of time to pray and get his thoughts together before service. All of us did, actually. A preacher's family is so very important to a service, not just the preacher himself. Any kids in a preacher's family really ought to make sure that their hearts are in tune with God before service, just like their mom and dad.

We got to church just in time for the prayer room at 6:45. And then service started just a minute or two after seven o'clock, and it was amazing. The Emmanuel Baptist Church, among other things, has a fantastic youth choir.

All of them sing well, and all of them sing with all of their hearts.

And then, after the offering, it was time for dad to preach. He preached one of my favorite messages, "Choosing Your Final Destination." It is mostly a salvation message, and we got to rejoice as, during the invitation, a gentleman came up to be saved. Man, that never gets old!

There was a lot of hugging and crying around the altar as the pastor took over the service to close it out. I could tell dad was really tired; he puts everything into all of his messages, but especially into that one.

After service, all of us and the pastor's family, and several others from church went over to McDonald's for a late supper and some ice cream. Mind you, we only got the supper, not ice cream, since, of course, "the ice cream machine is broken."

If only the entire world was so consistent and predictable.

It started to get kind of late, and all of the parents there got that look in their eyes that let all of us kids know the fellowship was coming to an end. Sure enough, within a few minutes, there were hugs and handshakes and goodbyes, and we made our way back to the Comfort Inn and Suites.

We climbed the stairs, got to our rooms, and then all of us met in mom and dad's room for our nightly conversation and prayer time. I know I have told you this before, but that is absolutely my favorite time of the day. Carrie's and Aly's too.

Finally, we hugged and said good night, and we three kids made our way into our room, knowing that we would not be there long.

Chapter Eight

I wish, oh how I wish it had been once again the cold of the snow on our cheeks that awakened us out there in the wilderness of Virginia. But though the snow was everywhere and far deeper than the night before, it was the screams and cries of anguish from the camp that awakened us on this dreadful day.

We knew without having to ask that the Winter Wolf, as we had begun to call him, had returned.

Instantly we were on our feet and rushing through the knee-deep snow through the trees, with the heavy-laden pine boughs slapping us as we went.

We burst out in the open and were stopped dead in our tracks. Two older ladies were kneeling over the two bodies of the two old men who had so graciously agreed to guard Mrs. Susan and baby Thomas last night. Those ladies were wailing in anguish, and I knew that the third voice that I was hearing wail was Mrs. Susan from inside the wagon itself.

Carrie and Aly rushed up onto the seat of the wagon and entered it from there so as not to have to cross over those dead bodies or those grieving widows. Trembling and horrified, feeling weak at the knees, I made my way over to the scene of the attack. Naturally, it was Lucky and Chubby who met me there.

"We can't outrun them; that is now pretty obvious, I would think," the leathery old man said with a shake of his head.

Chubby started to say something, but Lucky simply held up his hand to his face and said, "Not now."

"We need to get rid of them!" the fat man shrieked, and faster than I could have imagined, Lucky had backhanded him across the face. Chubby dropped to one knee, spitting blood. Immediately, though, he looked up at the man who had just struck him and said, "That's it, let's make each other bleed to attract them even more. Let's let the baby cry and the mama wail, and let's all of us bleed and die because of them. That's what we all came out here for, right?" He said sarcastically.

Lucky just whirled away from him and said, "Follow me, boy, if you want to see what we are up against."

The man walked to the western side of the wagon circle, the direction we were all traveling, and kept right on walking past the wagons and three hundred yards or so further out. Then he stopped, pointed down the ground, and simply said, "Look."

Once again, it took me a moment to process what I was seeing because it just did not seem natural at all. There seemed to be dozens of sets of wolf prints, but all of them were from normal-sized wolves. The Winter Wolf had not been here with them. But what was really surprising was that all of those sets of prints were lined up as if they had been arranged by a drill sergeant.

"They lined up here and started howling like the hounds of hell. It was so dark that we obviously could not see them to get off any clear shots, so we just shot at the awful sound.

Obviously, we did not hit a single one of them. But that still isn't the end of this story."

He turned and walked back toward the camp, and I had a hunch what I was going to see when we got there.

The two ladies were still grieving and weeping over their husband's bodies. Lucky went to them and said, "Laura, Martha, I'm so very sorry. Your husbands were good men, and good friends to me. But I need you two to go back to your wagons right now while we try to sort all of this out."

At that, some of the other ladies herded those wailing ladies away from the bodies of their husbands and toward one of the other wagons.

Lucky just stood there for a minute staring at those bodies; I could see the conflict raging within him.

"I wasn't just saying all of that. I have known both of these men for more than forty years. They were men to ride the river with. And that... demon, that Beelzebub from the pit, targeted and killed them for no good reason."

He did not have to explain to me what he meant. But he did so anyway.

"He left the bodies. Rather than dragging them off to eat, he simply killed both of them and left them laying here as some kind of a message to us. And in order to be able to do that, all of the other wolves were out front causing a distraction. That wolf is not normal; if I didn't know better, I would swear that it thinks and reasons like a man... or a devil."

I had absolutely nothing to say, mostly because I agreed with every word he said. I absolutely could not have put it any better myself.

"Three good men are dead, and everyone else is scared to death," he said angrily. "And every bit of it is because of that crying baby."

Before I could even ask, he answered.

"No, we aren't going to put them out—at least not yet," he said as he spat on the ground. "We still have a few tricks up our sleeves. Today we ride for half a day. We move out, and we move hard. But first, we bury our dead."

It took an hour of backbreaking work for all of us men and boys put together to dig through the snow and icy ground and get to shallow grave spots ready. Some of the ladies made some crude grave markers and even carved the names of those two heroic men into them.

"It's kind of sad," Aly said as she slipped up behind me during one of the moments when I was taking a break and letting someone else dig, "those grave markers will be rotted and gone within two or three years. No one in our day will ever know the brave men who lay here and the sacrifice they made."

"Nope, afraid not," I said. "But do you know who will know? Or, I should say, who does know? Every angel on the streets of glory and every hero of the faith from Noah to David to Daniel to the apostle Paul knows. Those men gave their lives for a mama and baby; I guarantee you all of heaven rose to welcome them home when they got there."

When the burial was done and the grave markers in place, Lucky stood, took off his hat, and spoke to everyone.

"Timothy and John were my friends. More than that, they were the ones who led me to Christ. I was a worthless drunk, and they hounded me and loved me and prayed for me until I got saved. And while I ain't been perfect since then, far from it, them two have always steered me toward God and the ways of God.

"I just wish I could be half the Christian that either of them were.

"The world may never know them, but we will never forget them."

And with those short, simple words, he turned to walk away and said, "And now we ride."

As we had a day earlier, we rode as if Satan himself were chasing us.

Both Aly and Carrie were beside me on the front seat as we raced across the wilderness. The terrain was a bit clearer today, and every wagon and driver there pushed the horses so hard that I was surprised they could live through it. The lovely firs of the high altitudes seemed to be fewer and fewer, and snow-covered maples and oaks seemed to dominate the scenery this day, though that was not much more than a passing thought to me as we sped along.

"Kyle, I'm worried," Aly said as she nestled closer beside me.

"What about, Squirt? I mean, other than the fact that we and all these people are being chased by some monster wolf?"

"Right now they are trying to protect Sarah and Thomas. But I'm afraid it won't take much more for them to put them out in the cold. That baby will die out here if that happens -- and he's just starting life."

I nodded.

"I know what you mean, Littlest Sis. And I'm glad you feel that way. Anyone with a heart should put innocent children at the top of the list of those to be protected at all times. That is why I can never understand people who think abortion is okay. Jesus actually had His disciples bring little children to Him so He could pick them up in His arms, and dad always says that important religious figures of that day never lowered themselves to do that. He was pretty much the only one who understood how precious they were, rather than viewing them as a nuisance.

"But let's not give up hope just yet. God sent us here for a reason, and He will help us fulfill that reason.

"The Night Heroes will do what it takes to take care of that baby."

We rode on in silence for a while, and at one point, it seemed as if the sun might possibly peek through the constant wall of gray clouds and give us a glimmer of light and hope in the midst of all of the shadows. But those clouds quickly regathered, and the snow began to fall again, harder than ever.

"It never stops, does it?" Carrie asked matter-of-factly.

"No, but apparently we do," I said as I heard the "All stop!" come echoing from the lead wagon. It was, by my guess, probably two o'clock in the afternoon. If that was accurate, we had about five hours till dark. We were about to find out what Lucky had up his sleeve to deal with this devilish wolf and his pack.

"Circle up, and make it tight!" was the next shout that came from up front, which was quickly followed by, "All men..." and then after a pause, "and any women of strength, too, grab axes and follow me."

Carrie and Aly looked at each other, and I knew what was coming next from Aly without even having to guess.

"THAT'S what I'm talkin' about!" she shouted as she fist-pumped four or five times. "Girl power to the rescue!"

I just shook my head and grinned.

We got our wagon in place, secured the horses, grabbed the ax from the back, and met Lucky and the other men and a couple of women up front.

"Listen close, people. We need logs about as thick as a man's arm, ten feet or so in length, and we need a bunch of them. And every one needs to have one end sharpened to a fine point. We also need smaller branches cut into two-foot lengths and sharpened. So, some of you cut, some of you haul, some of you sharpen. And I need four men with me to start arranging them. Go!"

Within ten seconds, everyone was divided into groups, and we were racing to the task. Carrie and Aly and a quiet young man of about twenty years old were with me.

"What is he up to, Kyle?" Carrie asked as we raced toward our first target tree.

"I suspect he is about to build an X-style barricade. The bigger stakes will be crossed and tied in the middle; the smaller ones will be used to stake them into the ground. It's a pretty good plan; I am guessing that wolf would have to jump about eight feet up and twelve feet over to clear both sides of the spikes."

Carrie scrunched up her forehead for a minute, and I knew what was coming. Sure enough, ten seconds or so later, she said, "Actually, it's more drastic than that. Bare minimum, on a pretty steep arch, he would have to go ten feet high and thirteen feet out. If he chose to use speed as his ally and take a smoother arch, like a clean semi-circle, it would be a ten-foot-high jump at the peak clearing more than twenty feet in length."

"Okay, great plan, then. Surely that werewolf wannabe can't pull off that jump. Let's get to work."

And we did, with a life-or-death urgency.

You know that we Night Heroes are no strangers to hard work and breathtaking activity. I could feel my muscles burning as I ripped through one sapling after another. The other guy was doing pretty good too, but to be honest, I was staying way ahead of him. The girls, for their part, were grabbing and hauling them back to camp like full-grown men.

"You and your sisters are good workers," the other guy said as he stopped a minute to catch his breath. "You must have a good Ma and Pa."

I smiled at that. It was interesting to consider his thought process, mostly because of how accurate it was. If a "Ma and Pa" are good, they absolutely teach their kids how to work hard. My dad always says, "If you don't teach a kid how to work, you teach him how to be lazy, and if you teach him how to be lazy, you teach him to be a thief."

"We do have a good Ma and Pa, absolutely. And yes, they have taught all of us to work. Let's just hope between all of us it will be enough."

"Uh huh," he grunted as he hoisted his ax again, "I sure don't want me or nobody else dying out here tonight."

We went back to work with a vengeance and pretty soon heard the dinner bell ring out from camp. Only all of us knew that it was not a call to come eat but a call to come build. Apparently, we had enough stakes to work with.

We rushed back to camp and saw the barricade well under way and jumped in to help. Over and over again, two sharpened poles would be stood up, crossed like an X, tied, turned sideways with one point facing out and the other facing in, and stakes would be driven into the ground to hold them in place. All of them were joined together, and just about the time night fell, we hung a hastily made yet heavy and strong wooden-stake gate in the small opening, and then a second one several feet further back. This made it sort of like the gates of ancient cities, allowing it to be the strongest point of the defense, yet at the same time allowing us in or out as needed.

Some of the ladies had a good fire going, and we could smell the lovely aroma of beans and cornbread, but definitely no meat. There would be nothing cooked that a wolf may like the smell off.

"Come eat, everybody." It was Lucky's voice, and we were glad to hear it. I knew that everyone's muscles were aching and stomachs were growling.

We carried our tools and sledgehammers to the center of the small camp, stacked them up, and sat down. The ladies brought each of us simple bowls of the amazing meal, we said grace, and everyone dug in.

I suspected that normally, on a wagon train, there would be happy talking, laughter, and even music as the lovely flames did their dance against the backdrop of the falling night and shimmering snow. But on this night, all was utterly silent save for the occasional clinking of a spoon against a dish. The weather was getting colder, much colder. And, as hard as we had worked and as well as we had prepared, I still did not have any confidence that any of this would work. I sure hoped it did – I just wouldn't have ever bet on it.

As we cleared the last few beans and crumbs off of our plates, the girls and I made eye contact. I nodded, handed them my plate, and got up. I brushed myself off, cornbread crumbs falling into the snow. *Hopefully, some bird can get a winter snack*, I thought to myself.

As I made my way over to Lucky, he clearly knew why I was coming.

"It's a bad idea," he said simply. "Anyone outside of this enclosure tonight will be at risk."

"I understand that, Sir," I said calmly. "But it's a risk we are willing to take. Besides, if we can make some noise and get a few miles away from the enclosure, maybe they will follow us instead of trying to get in."

He just looked at me as if he couldn't believe what he was hearing.

"You seriously intend to make yourselves bait to try and save us?"

"Yes sir, that's exactly what we intend."

"Boy, you and your sisters are about as crazy as possums swimmin' in a moonshine still – but I respect your courage."

I went and got Carrie and Aly and quickly told them what I had in mind. We knew that at some point, we had to get to sleep for our nightly trip back to our time, but in the meantime, we legitimately wanted to try to draw those wolves away.

Could we possibly lose our lives?

Yep.

But would we go down without a fight?

Not a chance.

We got our packs loaded up with blankets, a bit of food, knives, and other essentials. Then lucky gave each of us a rifle, walked us to the gate, and the men he had posted as guards opened both of them up for us. We walked through them, into the ever-darkening night, and both gates ominously slammed and fastened behind us.

We walked to the edge of the woods and then clicked on our small LED lights, confident they could not be seen from the camp. All three of us carried rifles, muskets, actually, since they were the "rifles" of the day. I quickly showed the girls how to use them and then said, "Are you ready?"

"You know it, Kyle," Aly said confidently. "Let's be the baddest bait on the block."

Carrie and I busted out laughing at that. I put a hand on her shoulder and said, "Okay, Pipsqueak, just be careful. Careless bait gets eaten, and that is not the outcome we are going for here."

And then, at the count of three, all three of us shouted at the top of our lungs and started running through the woods like crazed Indians. If there were any wolves anywhere near, they could not help but hear us.

We ran for four hours, alternating between making noise and trying to catch our breath. I figured that, with the snow slowing us down, we had covered maybe five miles.

"Okay, guys," I said as I pulled up to a stop, "that's as far as we go. We have to get to sleep so that we can wake up and spend the day with mom and dad in our time. Not showing up in the morning would be a pretty bad thing, I think. And either the wolves have followed us, or they haven't. If they have, then they are waiting for us to settle down and go to sleep so they can kill and eat us.

"But if that is the case, they are going to be pretty disappointed to find out that their prey has disappeared. Let's pack it in for the night."

And we did, as three tired, half-hoarse Night Heroes knelt to pray together and then wrapped up in our blankets under a tree, clutched our guns and packs tightly to our chests so we could carry them back to our time with us, and immediately fell fast asleep.

CHAPTER TEN

The knocking on the door between our rooms was clearly a dad knock, not a mom knock. I often wondered how door hinges held up when dad was around.

"Up and at 'em, sleepy heads!" came his booming voice, "daylight's wasting!"

"Ugghhhh. Why does he always have to be so... AWAKE every morning?" Aly groaned.

"No joke," Carrie added in agreement. "It's almost like he has no appreciation for kids who may or may not have spent most of last night running through the snow being chased by wolves."

All of us stowed our rifles under the couch where they would not be found if anyone came into the room. We wanted to carry them with us so that we could hopefully wake up closer to camp than the four or five miles we had run from it last night.

Aly made her way into the restroom to get ready while Carrie and I took time to read our Bibles. Then it was Carrie, then me, and finally we were all dressed and headed down to breakfast. But instead of breakfast at the hotel, this time breakfast would be at the Cracker Barrel just down the road.

I suppose it is possible that someone somewhere reading this has never heard of a Cracker Barrel. If so, I feel sorry for you. Cracker Barrel is an amazing restaurant/country store combination. There are games and gifts and toys and cool clothes, and candy and sodas from even way before our parent's time. But above all, there is food, great food, and lots of it.

It only took us a few minutes to wheel the trusty old Yukon into the parking lot. And then we piled out and headed for the front door, right under the huge front porch and past the rocking chairs and huge checker games on barrels. Once we got inside and got our names on the list, it only took us about twenty minutes to get a seat, and it was pretty close to the roaring open fireplace.

The waitresses at Cracker Barrels always seem to be so nice. That "down-home southern vibe," as Aly calls it. With a "Sugar" here and a "Honey" there, our orders were soon taken, and we settled into family time, talking about the day.

"So, you guys up for a little adventure to shake you out of your boring little lives?" Dad asked with a grin.

And for the second time this week, Aly got choked up and had to hold up a hand to let mom know she didn't need the Heimlich Maneuver.

Dad just looked at her like she was weird and continued on. "Not too far from here is the Virginia Creeper Trail."

"Um, no offense, Dad, but does anyone really need any more creeps or creepiness in their lives?" Carrie asked with a bit of concern.

"Not creeps or creepiness, Creeper Trail," mom corrected. "It is a thirty-five-mile bike trail through forests, across old train trestles; I hear it is amazing. The part we would do is all downhill, too."

"Downhill? Like, not having to peddle and huff and puff?" Carrie asked a bit too excitedly.

Dad just laughed.

"That is correct, my studious child, downhill. As in, 'let gravity do the job for you.' "

There was not a single negative vote on that one. I personally hate riding bikes, and I know dad does too. Running? Check. Lifting weights? Any day. But sitting on those hard, tiny, uncomfortable seats and pedaling around the block? Nope. No good reason for that. But if a person could simply ride downhill and enjoy the amazing scenery of the Virginia mountains and meadows, sign me up!

Our food arrived (Uncle Herschel's Favorite for dad, as always), and we dug in. There were mountains of pancakes, eggs, biscuits, apple butter, bacon, grits, just everything that mine exploring, pirate fighting, terrorist battling, wolf hunting boys and girls need.

There was also the triangle-shaped peg game in the middle of the table that every last one of us have memorized and can do perfectly every single time.

We all ate until we were full, and no one got in a hurry. Family time around the table is some of the most amazing time of every day.

Finally, though, we were finished up and ready to go bike riding. Mom paid the bill, and all of us waddled back out to the vehicle. A few minutes later, we were pulling into one of the local bike/shuttle shops, and we all went inside to rent the bikes and helmets and all of the necessary gear. Once that was done, we loaded up into a shuttle and started heading for Whitetop, the starting point for the part of the Virginia Creeper Trail that we would be doing, which would actually be about seventeen miles. It would end in Damascus, Virginia, where another shuttle would load us up and bring us back.

This was going to be epic.

It took about forty-five minutes to get to our starting point. But after that, it only took about five minutes for us to get going; none of us Warners are prone to be slow about things like that.

And man, what an awesome ride!

In the seventeen miles between the starting point and our ending point in Damascus, Virginia, the Creeper Trail descends right at 1500 feet. In other words, is steep enough to keep you from having to peddle 99% of the time, but not so steep that you have to worry about getting going too fast, smashing into something and falling off and breaking a bone. Not that a steep, fast trail would be anything that we Warner's or we Night Heroes would shy away from. Not in the least.

For many years the trail was actually an old rail line. But the last train ran there in 1977, and in the years that followed, people converted it to a hiking and biking trail. If you ever get to ride it, I promise you, you will never forget it. It meanders down a gravely path through beautiful forests, across a great many old trestle bridges, and some really long narrow wooden bridges, some of which are really high in the air!

The trail parallels a beautiful river a lot of the way, and then at several points crosses back and forth over top of it. There are a whole bunch of places to stop along the way to rest and take pictures and just enjoy the beauty of God's scenery. There are also a few places along the way that you can stop and eat or get work done on your bike if necessary.

"Try to keep up, Slowpoke" Aly said laughing as she sped by me, then by Carrie, then by mom, then by dad.

Well now, that was just never going to do...

I quickly started pedaling faster, kicking my speed into overdrive. I raced past Carrie and mom and dad and had Aly in my sights about seventy or eighty feet ahead.

"Take it easy, you two!" Mom said with a concerned tone in her voice.

"Let 'em go, Babe," dad said calmly, "they will either break some bones or they won't."

Thanks, dad.

It took me about a minute to breeze by my energetic little sister. And then I really started pushing hard and left her and everyone else in the dust – until I came to a crossroads. One direction said Creeper Trail, and the other direction said Appalachian Trail.

I slid to a stop and waited for everyone else to catch up, and in just a couple of minutes, they did so.

"What's up, Kyle?" Dad asked.

"The sign, Appalachian Trail," I said. "Is that the same Appalachian trail we were right near to when we were down in Hiawassee, Georgia?"

"It is," he said. "In fact, it starts not too far from there. It runs from Springer Mountain in Georgia to Mount Katahdin in Maine. That trail is about 2,200 miles long and takes around six months to hike.

"But that isn't what's really impressive," he said.

"Seriously?" I asked. "What do you mean?"

"What's really impressive," he said with a smile, "is how quickly I can put you in my rearview mirror."

And then he was off like a shot, pedaling like a speed demon.

"Oh, I don't think so!" I shouted, and then took off after him.

"Boys!" I heard Carrie say in a frustrated voice.

"Let them go," mom said. "They will either break some bones or they won't..."

About two hours later we all pulled into the parking lot of The Hellbenders Café. A hellbender, by the way, is a pretty large aquatic salamander found in those parts.

By the time we got there, we had all burned off breakfast pretty good. But in short order, we were sitting in front of huge corndogs, hamburgers, hot dogs, and mom had a chicken salad wrap. And then we topped everything off with ice cream. For the record, the raspberry chocolate chip is to die for.

But we knew we had to go ahead and finish the trail and get back to the hotel to get ready for service tonight. And so, we bid a fond farewell to a new favorite food place and headed the rest of the way down into Damascus, ending up at the Sundog Outfitter. The shuttle bus met us there and took us back to our vehicle. A few moments later, we pulled into a Dollar General for snacks and supplies. The girls and I intentionally grabbed what we needed pretty quickly, checked out while mom and dad were still shopping, and went back out to the vehicle. Then a few moments later, they joined us, we got on the road, and shortly, we were pulling back into the hotel.

The next couple of hours were the standard routine of showers (which we all desperately needed by that point) and dressing and poofing and primping, followed by a bit of quiet time to get our hearts prepared for the night service.

Then we all loaded up one more time and made our way back to the lovely Emmanuel Baptist Church.

As always, all of the congregational singing was heartfelt and lovely, and all of the special singing and the adult choir singing was impeccably well done. But it was not a "performance;" all of it was a heartfelt offering of praise to the Lord.

I often sit in services like that and hear the beautiful singing and see the tears of joy flowing and imagine that heaven is going to be a lot like that. Can you imagine how great the worship services will be when none of us ever get tired or sick or sinful or bored or distracted, and the One that we are singing about is actually sitting on the throne for us to see with our eyes? Man, if I was lost, I would sure want to get saved, just for that, if nothing else!

I snapped back to attention when I heard the pastor announcing my dad one more time and asking him to come preach.

And, as always, he preached with all of his heart. This time he preached a message from Joshua 7 called "Get Up!" The gist of it is that Joshua and the children of Israel had such a great success at the battle of Jericho – and then turned right around and failed miserably when trying to defeat the tiny city of Ai. Joshua, their leader, fell on his face to the ground and was actually whining and moaning out loud.

And God told him to get up.

A lot of times it's sort of amazing to me to think how complicated we make things. If you have fallen, the simplest thing to do is get back up. The whole message was basically about that. God never expects us to lay there in our failures or even in our hard circumstances and whine and moan. People who lay down and quit never do succeed, and they certainly never win. But if you will just make up your mind to always get back up when you fall or fail, then you will accomplish great things in your life and great things for God.

It was a really encouraging message, and during the invitation, the altar was full of people crying and praying.

After service, we went with the pastor's family back down to Bristol to Ruby Tuesday. It was late, so all of us just got salads. Eating heavy meals late is rarely a good idea. But the food was good, and the fellowship was even better.

Finally, though, it was time for us to pack things in for the night. So we said our goodbyes, our family prayed with theirs, and we loaded up and headed back down the road to our hotel. In short order, we were all ready for our nightly family conversation and prayer time. And then when that was done, we said our good nights, and the girls and I went to our room. When we got there, we loaded our packs with a few extra things to help us in our battle against this awful wolf.

And then we prayed a very specific and important prayer.

Lord, if you don't mind, could you please allow us to wake up close to camp? We want to be there for them as quickly as possible. If you could help us with this, we would sure appreciate it, and we pray it in Jesus' name, amen.

CHAPTER ELEVEN

Gunshots. And right nearby. My heart jumped into my throat as all three of us Night Heroes jumped to our feet and took off running. All of us knew that our prayer from last night had been answered; the noise told us we could not be more than a hundred yards or so from camp.

We broke out into the open just a few yards from the enclosure – and absolutely could not believe our eyes when we saw what we saw.

It was our first actual glimpse of the Winter Wolf. In broad daylight.

He was airborne.

Coming from inside the enclosure.

He completely cleared it; it was an incredible jump. And since he was coming from the inside, I knew that he had already made that jump once.

As soon as his paws hit the ground, the girls and I unloaded on him with our muskets – and all three shots missed the mark as he bobbed and weaved like lightning, heading for the trees on the other side of the meadow. But when he got to them, I am not making this up, he stopped and turned and looked at us, and it was the most evil look on the face of any animal that I have ever seen.

Then he rared his head back, howled an unearthly howl that seemed to shake the ground under our feet, and took off into the forest. I could see several shapes joining him in the trees, and I knew he and his pack were now out of our reach yet again.

The only question was, what damage had been done this time.

We shouted for someone to open the gate, and quickly they did. Aly and Carrie immediately rushed for Susan's wagon.

"Did you hit him?!?" Chubby screamed, "Did you hit him?!?"

"No!" I shouted back, "All three of us tried. We all had him dead in our sights, and he dodged each and every shot. Did he get anybody?"

The fat man's face got redder than ever.

"Did he get anybody? Did he get anybody?!? Yeah, boy, he got somebody. He got the most important somebody we have."

It was Lucky.

I dropped my head in anguish and defeat. That man was the glue that held this entire motley wagon train together. He didn't have enough meat on his leathery body to even be interesting to that wolf. If it was about food, he would have cleared that fence and immediately gone for Chubby. That creature knew who his main adversary was and specifically targeted him.

Finally, I looked back up and said, "I'm so sorry for your loss. He was a good man. I guess I have to ask, who's in charge now, and what will you all do?"

I suspected I was not going to like the answer.

I was right.

"I'm in charge now, that's who. And I'll blame sure tell you what we're not going to do; we're not gonna lose any more men over that crying baby."

"You can't put Mrs. Susan and that child out into the wilderness alone; they won't survive!" Aly shouted angrily as she showed up holding the baby.

"Well, you don't need to worry about that mama, at least," the fat man said with a sneer. "She died last night, which is why you found that kid alone in the wagon. And her death was none too soon, if you ask me, since she's the one that brought this problem down on us to begin with."

As quick as lightning, I made him regret that filthy statement. With a compact right hook I busted him in the side of the face and dropped him to the ground. That was the second time on this journey he had found himself like that.

I should have known what was coming next. Chubby shook his head, trying to clear the cobwebs, and finally, he managed to stand. The heavy, fast-falling snow was oh, so cold. But nowhere near as cold as the dozen or so rifle barrels pointing right at us.

"If you want to try and keep this baby alive, then take it and go. But under no circumstances can it stay with us a single minute longer. The more it cries, the more of these wolves keep coming, especially that ungodly monster leading the pack. Enough of these men have died already, and no one else among us is going to do so if I can help it."

I looked over at Carrie and Aly and immediately had my answer. The looks on their faces as they mothered that precious, helpless babe let me know that we would save it or die trying.

So come on ahead, wolf; the Night Heroes will be ready for you.

CHAPTER TWELVE

Chubby and the entire wagon train, at least what was left of it, were gone. They were "kind" enough to leave me a shovel with which I was presently digging, or lease attempting to dig, a grave for Mrs. Susan. Clearing the snow had not been that hard of a thing; digging a big enough hole in the frozen ground was another matter.

It took me about two hours. During that time, the girls had started a small fire and were warming up some formula for the baby. That and a bottle from our Dollar General stop were some of the things we brought with us our pack last night, just in case it was needed.

And then came the hardest part of all.

The girls had wrapped Mrs. Susan up in a blanket. While Aly held little Thomas and fed him, Carrie and I placed the body gently into the grave I had dug. Then we covered her up, and I have to admit I cried as I did. I have been to funerals before – but I have never had to be the one to put a body in the ground and cover it up.

Once we had her covered up with the dirt, I built a hasty wooden grave marker and carved her name into it. I drove it into the ground and just hoped that someone would find it come spring and know who was buried here.

Then it was time to put our plan into action. For the record, none of us really liked it – but it seemed to be the only thing that made any sense whatsoever.

"Is everybody ready, and is everybody up for this?" I asked. The girls nodded grimly, and I nodded back. Then we put the most important part of the plan into action; we prayed.

"Lord, we really do need your help. A lot of lives have been lost so far, and we don't want any more of that to happen. Please protect those folks on the wagon train, even though they left us and a baby alone in the snow to die. Lord, they are just scared, and they are acting on that fear. When you were on the cross, you prayed, 'Father, forgive them, for they know not what they do.' I am praying the same thing right now concerning them. I'm mad at them, sure. But I know that if they were thinking straight, they wouldn't have done this, and I know that you love them and died for them.

"Please protect us and little Thomas, too. I can't exactly punch that wolf in the nose to try and beat it. If you don't give us the wisdom to handle that thing, then none of us will live out the night. Please let this plan work, and please, please, please bring us all back safely together at the end of it.

"I pray all of this in Jesus' name, amen."

The last thing any of us wanted to do was split up. But if we were going to save that baby, it was our only hope. Carrie's research told us that there was a small town about ten miles south of our present location. In that time and in that remote wilderness, that may as well have been a continent away. But if she was right, that is where we could find the help we needed. So, she was going to be heading that direction; Aly and I were going to be going the exact opposite direction, due north. We hoped to make it to one of the limestone caves that are so common that near to the Blue Ridge Mountains.

It was sort of crazy, really. What fourteen-year-old girl gets sent out into the snow of the wilderness by herself? But all of us knew that it was God who always equipped us for the task, and we just trusted Him to make us ready and capable.

We all hugged each other really tight, and Carrie said, "Don't worry about me. You two just watch out for each other, and I'll plan on seeing you back in the hotel room later on."

There was nothing more to be said, so she took off running to the south, and we took off running north. And all the while, I could hear the soft baby whimpers coming from the pack strapped carefully and tightly to my back.

"Let's go hard and fast, Aly, the race to those caves is literally a life-or-death race right now."

We were really pushing hard. Normally we would have taken a few more breaks along the way, but we knew we simply couldn't afford it under the circumstances. And then we heard it;

the dreadful sound that we knew was eventually coming.

"I hate that stupid howling, and I hate that stupid wolf," Aly said as we picked up the pace.

"I know, Sis, me too. But we knew that even the daylight wouldn't stop them from coming after us. They are following the sound of the baby, just like we knew they would. Run faster, and just keep running."

All day long, we raced against time. The sound of the howling was getting slightly closer, and yet I knew that if they really wanted to, they could have already run us down. They were intentionally howling behind us to push us harder and to exhaust us. They fully intended to run us into the ground and then eat us at their leisure.

And that thought got me angry.

And sometimes, anger is a very good motivator.

"Let's pick up the pace a little more, Littlest Sis. Those dog-faced pet store rejects expect us just to give up and lay down for them. Let's disappoint them in a big way."

Aly actually growled when I said that. That brought a smile to my face. Count on the youngest Night Hero; when energy and emotion is needed, she will come through with it.

Hey, this is Carrie; I'll pick my part of the story up from here.

I was praying hard for my big brother and little sister as they raced north. Sure, we often fight just like regular brothers and sisters, but any of us would die for the other without blinking an eye.

Though I was in a hurry and kept slipping and falling, always careful to twist and land on my face rather than my back, I could not help but be in awe of the winter wonderland around me. The snow on the ground in the boughs and branches of every tree was acting like a sound muffler; it was as if I was all alone in the world. And yet, I knew that the wolf pack and the Winter Wolf were still very much out there. Thus far, it seemed like they were following Kyle and Aly, just as we suspected they would. And that meant I had to hurry and get to help before they could get to them.

I pushed ahead hard, my pack securely strapped to my back. The terrain before me was gradually going downward, and I could not help but think of the Creeper Trail that we had so gently cruised down just a few hours ago and hundreds of years from now.

But there would be no bicycle wheels to get me where I needed to go today. If I made it, it would be because I kept on putting one foot in front of the other and getting back up each and every time I fell down, just like dad said in his message last night.

Though the sun in the sky was, as usual in this adventure, completely hidden behind an impenetrable ceiling of clouds, south was not hard to find. This, of course, was due to my handy dandy compass. Great tool, that. A GPS would never work in the 1780s, but the magnetic field was up and running from the day God made this lovely blue ball called Earth that we live on.

Try as I might, I could not seem to go as fast as I wanted to. The weight on my back, plus the slipping and sliding of the downhills, was really slowing me down. "Lord," I prayed, "please give me better traction; I could really use it."

And then I fell again.

You know, sometimes the Lord answers our prayers just the way we would like Him to. But He is, in fact, God. And this means that sometimes He absolutely doesn't answer our prayer just the way we would like Him to.

When He says yes, praise Him. When He says no, praise Him anyway.

I got back up, brushed off my face, and kept going. And then I prayed again.

"Lord, even if I fall thousand times, help me to get to where I need to be for this to work. And please keep Kyle and Aly safe. Give them the traction that I don't seem to have."

This is Kyle; I'll pick it back up again from here.

Aly and I were doing surprisingly well making our way through the snow; our pace for the last little bit was far better than I had expected, almost like we had found our second wind. We had reached the bottom of the mountain that we had been aiming for. I was pretty confident we could find some suitable cave partway up it if God would just give us the strength to climb and eyesight to see.

We started our climb, still aware of the whimpering sounds coming from my pack.

The wolves were still aware of it as well; their howls were getting closer than ever.

"Climb, Sis, climb hard!" I said with urgency.

And both of us did.

Climbing up the side of a moderately steep mountain in the best of times in dry conditions would be at least a little bit difficult. But under these conditions, climbing through snow and ice, not able to see what was under that snow and ice, and with both of us absolutely, utterly exhausted, it was brutal. We fell on our faces over and over again but kept on scrambling upward. The howls of the wolves began to echo off the mountain face. They were closing in.

"Hurry, hurry!" Aly shouted. "There has to be a cave up here somewhere!"

My hands were bleeding from grasping at branches sticking above the snow to try to pull myself upward.

"Look!" I shouted as I pointed up ahead and to the left.

As if God Himself had opened a door for us in the mountainside, there was a cave opening about three hundred yards away.

The whimpering noises were still coming from my pack, and the howls were still coming from down below.

"One more big push, Sis, give it everything you have!" I shouted.

Pawing with our hands and feet like we were trying to swim up the mountainside, we finally pulled ourselves up and over a rock ledge and crawled on our hands and knees into a place that may as well have been heaven itself. It had been eight solid hours of nonstop running and climbing.

We had nothing left to give, but we knew we had to give it anyway.

"Kindling!" I shouted.

Aly dropped her pack, ripped the top open, and pulled out twigs and branches she had collected along the way. I quickly arranged them in the opening to the cave, yanked down some pine branches from scrubby trees around the mouth of the cave, and piled it all together.

"Lighter fluid and lighter!" I shouted again.

She already had those things in her hands. I squirted everything down and put the flame to it, and it roared to life.

"You know that won't last long, and when it dies, they're coming in," Aly said with a fearful tone in her voice.

"I know, Sis, I know. We've already talked about this. Make ready."

Hey everybody, this is Carrie again. Tears were streaming down my face; half of them tears of fear since night had fallen, the other half tears of joy as I could see candles in the windows of the tiny town just down below me. I ran for everything I was worth, knowing that time was absolutely of the essence, and precious life was hanging in the balance. "Please, God," I prayed, "please let me make it in time..."

Hey guys, this is Kyle one more time. The fire was dying; I knew we had just minutes left at best. I just prayed that Carrie had made it to town by now. Outside of the cave in the growing darkness of the waning light from the fire, I could see the evil glow of dozens of sets of green eyes... one of which stood much higher than the others. I could hear the growls and howls as the Winter Wolf called all of his pack to the prey. But, having already seen how he worked, I knew that when the fire died, he and he alone would enter the cave for what he deemed to be rightfully his. He had chased this baby across the wilderness, picking off protectors one at a time. If he had his way, Aly and I would be killed first; then he would have his tender morsel.

It was pure evil, birthed from the kennels of hell.

I was sitting against the back wall of the cave as the last flame flickered into embers.

And then I heard the click of claws as the Winter Wolf stepped over the remains of the fire and into the cave. I clicked on my small LED light and gasped. Even having seen it jump the enclosure fence did not do it the justice of seeing it close-up:

That. Thing. Was. Huge.

A low growl filled the cave. The baby whimpered yet again, and the wolf took another step closer. I just sat there calmly. What else was there to do? Another step... another step... another step... and then I slid the source of the whimpering across the floor to the waiting wolf.

He seemed surprised that the sound was coming from a cell phone instead of a baby, and the unknown item stopped him dead in his tracks.

And that was all I needed.

"Now!" I screamed.

Aly, hidden in the darkness in the side of the cave, pulled both triggers at the exact same time. How that tiny kid managed to hoist and fire both muskets at once is beyond me, but she did it. The blasts knocked her backward into the wall, and both shots hit that wolf broadside, knocking it into the other wall.

And instantly, I was on it, finishing it off with a hatchet.

And just like the Philistines of Goliath's day, when the other wolves saw that their "champion" was dead, they disappeared into the night.

Aly came running over to me. We looked at the dead wolf at our feet, the evil creature that had caused so much death and destruction. We held each other, cried a bit, and then prayed and thanked God for His help.

And at just that moment, many miles away, Carrie burst into the door of a tiny doctor's shanty and said, "This baby needs help right away. He has been asleep all day thanks to something called Benadryl that you have never heard of, but he isn't well and needs help."

A young doctor and his wife came running into the room, saw the baby, and gasped. The doctor reached for his bag, and his wife took the baby and said, "Whose baby is this, child? Surely you are too young to be the mother."

Carrie looked at the Bible on the small desk, smiled, and said, "Yours."

Then she walked away and out into the night.

Coming Soon

Desert Heat

The town of Columbus could hardly be considered a town anymore. Most of the buildings were burned to the ground and those that weren't were damaged so badly that they probably should be. The dead of both sides were being rounded up—the Americans for burial, the attackers for burning. It was the first, and so far the only invasion of the U.S. mainland in history, and it was led by Pancho Villa himself.

But Pancho Villa was not our concern. Not directly, at least.

"What happens now, Carrie?" I asked. "Break out the history on us, or, for this exact moment, the present."

"Well, within just a few hours, Major Frank Thompson will be taking about sixty men down into Mexico to chase him. He will battle with his troops, but he won't catch Villa. And then in about a week, General Blackjack Pershing will be taking a much larger force after him, and that will be an eleven-month attempt at catching him."

I nodded grimly.

"In other words," I said, "we have no time to lose. All of Mexico is about to be as hot as the surface of the sun, and a lot of people and things are about to get broken. If we don't get to that kid first, he may never make it home."

Other books in the Night Heroes Series

Cry From the Coal Mine (Vol. 1)
Free Fall (Vol. 2)
Broken Brotherhood (Vol. 3)
The Blade of Black Crow (Vol. 4)
Ghost Ship (Vol. 5)
When Serpents Rise (Vol. 6)
Moth Man (Vol. 7)
Runaway (Vol. 8)
Terror by Day (Vol. 9)

More Books by Dr. Bo Wagner

Beyond the Colored Coat
Don't Muzzle the Ox
From Footers to Finish Nails
I'm Saved! Now What???
Learning Not to Fear the Old Testament
Marriage Makers/Marriage Breakers

Daniel: Breathtaking
Esther: Five Feast and the Finger Prints of God
James: The Pen and the Plumb Line
Jonah: A Study in Greatness
Nehemiah: A Labor of Love
Romans: Salvation From A-Z
Ruth: Diamonds in the Darkness
Proverbs: Bright Lights from Dark Sayings

Devotionals

DO Drops Volume 1
DO Drops Volume 2
DO Drops Volume 3
DO Drops Volume 4
DO Drops Volume 5

Sci-Fi

Zak Blue and the Great Space Chase Series:
Falcon Wing (Vol. 1)
Enter the Malestrom (Vol. 2 Coming Soon!)